Lights Out

adapted by Jane Mason and Sara Hines Stephens
based on "Haunted House" written by Steve Holland
and "Broadcast Views" written by Anthony Del Broccolo

Based on *Zoey 101* created by Dan Schneider

SCHOLASTIC INC.

New York   Toronto   London   Auckland   Sydney
Mexico City   New Delhi   Hong Kong   Buenos Aires

ISBN 0-439-88259-1

© 2006 ApolloMedia.

Published by Scholastic Inc.

12 11 10 9 8 7 6 5 4 3 2   6 7 8 9 10/0

Printed in the U.S.A.

First printing, September 2006

Halloween High Jinks

It was a beautiful fall day on the Pacific Coast Academy campus. The air was warm, the sky was blue, and the crystal waves were lap, lap, lapping on the shore. On the patio overlooking the ocean, Zoey, Nicole, Chase, and Michael were enjoying the breeze and chowing down on some lunch. This was one of Zoey's favorite things about PCA — eating outside. Zoey tugged at the sleeve of her purple shirt, adjusting the large orange-and-pink brooch at her neck before turning her attention to her lunch. While Chase munched on a massive plate of french fries, Nicole and Zoey were savoring a couple of deli sandwiches.

"Okay, I have a question," Nicole said, holding up a green olive and squinting at it suspiciously.

"What's your question?" Zoey wanted to know.

Nicole examined the olive between her fingers.

No matter how much she studied the little thing, she could not figure it out. "What is the little red thing inside olives?" she asked.

Chase nodded knowingly. "Oh, it's the olive's tongue," he said, deadpan.

Nicole shrieked and tossed the olive into the bushes behind her. "Eww! Sick!" she squealed. She did not want any food that could taste her back.

Michael and Chase exchanged a look that said, "Good one." Nicole was so gullible, playing jokes on her was too easy, and way too hard to resist.

Michael grinned. "Hey, you asked," he pointed out.

Zoey smiled and shook her head at her friends. Sometimes Nicole was an easy target . . . but did she really believe that olives had tongues?

The guys were still laughing when Logan rolled up on his skateboard. "Wassup, peeps?" he greeted them casually, stepping off his board and tipping it with his foot into his outstretched hand.

Zoey munched a fry. "Hey, what happened to your arm?" she asked, pointing to the large white bandage on Logan's forearm.

Logan grinned mischievously. "Oh, I cut it really bad when I was jumping the fence behind the gym. See?" He carefully peeled the bandage back. Michael and Chase leaned in for a closer look, and a stream of bright red blood squirted from the wound, spewing all over Chase's pile of fries.

Chase and Michael jumped back and groaned while Nicole screamed like a victim in a horror movie. Even Zoey recoiled at the sight of the gore. But then, as more and more blood poured out and Logan started to laugh, she got a little suspicious. So did Michael.

He reached over and touched the blood — it was cold and felt like syrup. "Relax," he assured the girls. "That's fake blood."

Chase stared down at the blood-covered fries sitting in front of him, still looking horrified. "Yes. All over my french fries," he said, giving Logan a look. He liked a good joke as much as the next guy, but did the dude have to ruin his lunch?

Zoey rolled her eyes. Logan was cute — almost as cute as he thought he was — but he had a huge ego and could be totally immature. "Why are you walking around spewing fake blood out of your arm?" she asked, wondering if there could actually be a reason.

"Just testing out some new scares for this year's haunted house," he said, grinning. He was acting like he had invented the whole concept of fake blood himself.

Zoey raised her eyebrows. Even if Logan was so

full of himself he was in danger of popping, a haunted house sounded intriguing.

"What haunted house?" Nicole asked, beating her to the punch.

"Oh, see, every Halloween, the upper school does a haunted house for the lower school," Chase explained. He loved Halloween and the haunted house tradition. And he had a great costume lined up this year. . . .

"And this year? I'm in charge," Logan bragged.

Chase waved his arms, gesturing to all three of the guys at the table. "*We're* in charge," he reminded Logan.

Nicole bounced up and down in excitement, making her dangly earrings swing wildly. "Cool, I love haunted houses," she said. There was nothing better than getting a little spooked on Halloween. It was a great excuse to jump and grab the hand of the cute guy next to you.

"Me, too," Zoey agreed. "Can we help you guys set it up?"

Chase grinned. As far as he was concerned, any opportunity to spend time with Zoey was an opportunity worth taking. "Yes, you can help us set up the haunted house," he agreed with a nod.

Logan looked disgusted. Even after a full year, he still thought the PCA girls did not measure up to the guys. What was Chase thinking inviting them to help? "Dude —" he started to protest.

"Too late," Nicole said, cutting him off. "Chase said we could, so ha!" She couldn't help rubbing it in just a little. How many times would Logan have to learn that the PCA girls were just as good as, if not better than, the guys?

Michael eyed Logan. He was in no place to argue. "You've been 'ha'd,'" he pointed out, on the off chance that Logan missed it.

"By girls," Chase added, sitting back and giving Logan a satisfied nod.

Logan bristled and tried to shrug it off. "Whatever," he said. He acted like he didn't care. But if these girls thought they were going to come in and take over his haunted house, they had another thing coming. They could help out. "But this haunted house is gonna be majorly scary," he warned them. "Not girly scary." He emphasized the word *girly* and gave them all a look before hopping back onto his skateboard, pushing off, and disappearing into a crowd of students.

Chase watched him go, then stared down at his tainted fries. They looked completely disgusting, all soggy and slimed up with fake blood. "Hey, can I have a french fry?" he asked Zoey, gingerly picking up one from his plate and wrinkling his nose at it. "Mine are covered in Logan blood." He dropped the defiled fry and pushed the plate of offending fried potatoes away.

Zoey nodded. Chase's fries did look totally gross, and she was pretty sure they tasted even worse. "Sure." Zoey pushed her plate toward Chase just as a man and a woman in dress suits came up to their table.

"*Nous excuser. Nous sommes perdus,*" the man said in French. He looked totally perplexed.

"*Pouvez-vous nous diriger s'il vous plait au â timent d'administration?*" the woman added. They were obviously looking for help of some kind, but Zoey could not understand a word they had said.

Zoey smiled apologetically. "I'm sorry, we don't understand," she said.

Nicole leaned in close to Zoey. "I think they're foreign," she whispered.

Duh. Zoey shot Nicole a look.

She was looking around for someone who might know French when Mrs. Newsome, the foreign language teacher, came rushing up to them. "There you are!" she called excitedly. "There you are! I've been looking all over for you." She rushed up to the French couple, greeting them both with a peck on each cheek.

Zoey smiled, feeling relieved. She didn't have to

find a translator, but she still had no idea who these people were. "Who are they?" she asked Mrs. Newsome.

Mrs. Newsome smiled proudly. "Oh, this is Andre and Monique Jambon. They're teachers from a boarding school in France, here visiting PCA."

Andre and Monique smiled shyly, nodding hello.

"Oh, hey."

"Hi."

"Good to meet you," the kids greeted.

Zoey smiled a little wistfully. "I've always wanted to visit France," she offered.

"Yeah," Chase said, holding up one of Logan's fake-blood-covered fries. "We love your fries."

Andre reached down and took the fry from Chase's hand, gratefully accepting what looked like a generous offer of food. *"Ahhh, merci!"* he said smiling and nodding before popping it into his mouth.

"Wait . . ."

"Oh, no . . ."

"Not those . . ."

"Ewwww . . ." The kids all spoke at once, but it was too late.

Andre chewed happily . . . for about a second . . . before his face contorted into a look of total disgust.

CHAPTER 2

Setup and Getups

Just outside the science building, Michael opened the lid of one of the piled-up plastic tubs filled with Halloween stuff and started to sift through it. The haunted house was tonight, and they had lots to do to get ready. They were setting it up in the basement of the science building. Dark and filled with old lab equipment, it was the spookiest place on campus even before it was remade into a haunted house. When they were finished ghouling it up, it would be downright terrifying.

Michael pulled out a couple of monster heads and handed them to the dude who was helping him. He was just reaching back into the box when Logan came rushing out of the science building, holding a clipboard and looking annoyed. "Hey, I need those monster heads inside now," he ordered. "Let's go! Double time!"

Rolling his eyes, the guy holding the two heads

followed Logan inside. Michael groaned at his roommate while he opened another box filled with fake cobwebs and plastic tombstones. Logan was turning into a monster — and it wasn't his Halloween costume.

"Hey, Michael," a voice called out from behind him.

Michael turned around and saw Zoey's little brother, Dustin, and his roommate, Jack. They were two of the younger kids from the lower school — the ones the upper-school kids were making the haunted house for.

Raising his hand, Michael slapped Dustin and Jack each a high five. "Hey, little D, Jack. Happy Halloween, man."

"Thanks," Dustin replied, stepping over to check out the contents of one of the open crates. It was filled with really cool stuff like glowing spiders and prosthetics. "Oooh, is this some of the scary stuff for the haunted house —"

Logan ran up to Dustin. "Hey!" he growled, knocking a bloody ghoul's hand out of Dustin's grasp. "Unh-uh. Outta here." He shook his head. No way was letting the little kids go through the stuff allowed — it was supposed to be a surprise . . . a scary surprise.

Dustin stepped back and looked at Logan like he was nuts. Logan didn't have to get all freaked about it. "Why?" Dustin wanted to know.

Logan made a face. Hello! Was the kid dense? "'Cause I don't want you seeing any of the haunted house stuff till tonight," he said condescendingly. "So just take your little roommate and go." He waved his arm as if he were shooing away a pesky bug.

Jack gave Logan the eye. "Fine," he said, acting like he couldn't care less. "Haunted houses are stupid, anyway."

Dustin nodded emphatically. "Yeah, I've been to, like, ten haunted houses, and I've never been scared once," he boasted, looking up at Logan boldly through his shaggy blond bangs.

Logan took a step toward the younger boys menacingly. "Really?" he asked, leaning down so his face was very close to theirs. "'Cause, uhhh . . . this time, I'm in charge of the haunted house. And it's not just gonna make you scream. It's gonna make you cry."

Dustin stared up at Logan, trying not to shake in his shoes. Next to him, Jack's big brown eyes got bigger.

Logan gave the boys a last challenging look, then straightened up. Jack and Dustin stood frozen.

"C'mon, man." Michael whacked Logan on the shoulder. "Why ya gotta freak 'em out like that?" He stepped up to the younger boys. "Don't let him get you all scared," he said reassuringly. "He —"

"GWAAAAHHHHHHHHHHHH!!!" Logan roared from behind a terrifying rubber mask, lunging at Dustin, Jack, and Michael.

"Ahhhhhh!" Dustin jumped a foot and took off running, with Jack right behind him.

Panicked, Michael raced off in the other direction.

Logan pulled off the mask and grinned to himself as he watched them go. He was the coolest guy on campus *and* a haunted house master.

Zoey strolled across the PCA campus feeling totally Halloweeny. She and Nicole had just put the finishing touches on their costumes, and Zoey had to admit they looked great.

As they passed a circular fountain, they ran into their favorite teacher, Mr. Bender. He skidded to a halt right in front of them and nodded approvingly. "Wow. Whoa," he said, checking out their outfits.

Nicole did a little curtsy and grinned. "Hey, Mister Bender," she greeted, twirling one of her long dark ponytails.

"Whaddaya think?" Zoey added, smoothing her satiny 1950s-style white halter dress. She was wearing a short blond wig and heels to go with it. "Know who I am?"

Mr. Bender nodded. "I believe I do, Miss Marilyn Monroe."

Zoey grinned. Bingo.

"And how 'bout me?" Nicole asked, showcasing her blue gingham pinafore dress and red shoes.

Mr. Bender tapped a finger on his chin. "Let's see . . . might you be looking for the Yellow Brick Road?" he asked.

Nicole giggled. "Yes. See, I always wanted to be Dorothy for Halloween, but I wanna be scary, too, and Dorothy's not scary, so Zoey thought of a great idea. Look!" she said excitedly. Nicole spun around to reveal a large silver ax stuck in her back, complete with a bloody blade.

Mr. Bender chuckled. "Aha. So, you're Dorothy . . . but with an ax stuck in your back," he said.

Nicole turned back around and waggled a finger at the teacher. "Uh-huh," she agreed. Then she leaned in a little closer. "Can't trust that Tin Man," she said in a low voice before crossing her arms over her chest and shaking her head with mock sadness.

Mr. Bender nodded slowly, as if he understood perfectly. "Apparently," he agreed.

Eyeing Mr. Bender, Zoey suddenly realized that

he was also dressed up for Halloween. "Hey, we love your costume, too," she said.

Nicole nodded in agreement. "Yeah," she said.

Mr. Bender looked confused. "Costume?" he asked.

Nicole laughed. Mr. Bender was such a crack-up. "Yeah, the bow tie and the dorky shirt," she said, as if it weren't obvious already.

Zoey pointed to Mr. Bender's red plaid shirt and the colorful tie around his neck. "You're a nerd, right?" she guessed.

Mr. Bender nodded, looking a little embarrassed. "Right, yeah. I'm a big nerd," he agreed.

Zoey wondered why Mr. Bender seemed embarrassed about his costume. Didn't they just tell him it was a good one?

"Well, we gotta go help the guys set up the haunted house," Zoey said. She didn't want to miss any of the fun. It was going to be awesome!

Mr. Bender nodded, still looking a little funny. "Right."

Nicole gave a little wave. "Later!" she called as she and Zoey stepped around the teacher and continued up the path.

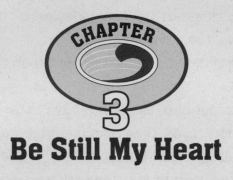

CHAPTER 3

Be Still My Heart

Across campus, the haunted house construction was in full swing. Pirates, surgeons, ghouls, and soldiers carried boxes of supplies into the science building basement. Tim, a mummy who was covered up to his neck in strips of graying cloth, loaded several large boxes onto a dolly.

Logan scowled and paced around, dressed as the grim reaper in a long black hooded robe and red gloves. He carried a scythe with a long curved blade and swung it impatiently. What was wrong with these people? Everything they did took forever! "C'mon, guys, we gotta hurry!" he barked. "It's gonna be dark in three hours!"

Zoey rolled her eyes at Logan as she and Nicole approached the building. Did he really think that harassing his helpers would make things go any faster?

They were almost to the door when Nicole gasped

and stopped in her tracks. "Oh, my God!" she squealed to Zoey.

Zoey stopped and looked around. She didn't see anything of "oh, my God" caliber. "What?" she asked, wondering what her friend was shrieking about.

"There's Tim," Nicole squeaked, grabbing Zoey's arm. "Look at him. Isn't he gorgeous? Say he's gorgeous."

Zoey shrugged. He was cute enough, but nothing to get all worked up over. Not that she'd tell Nicole that. "He's gorgeous," she agreed for her friend's sake.

Nicole nodded emphatically. "I know! And he's dressed as a mummy. That is *so* creative." She held up her hands to Zoey dramatically. "I must make him love me," she announced before scurrying closer to him.

Trying not to roll her eyes, Zoey followed her friend and Tim into the science building. Inside, the haunted house was really coming along. The cement walls were covered in black cloth. Cobwebs, skeletons, and life-size monsters were set up all over the place. Several guys were busy putting up even more. And at one end of the room, Zoey spied the entrance to a long, dark tunnel — the Tunnel of Doom. It all looked totally cool.

Halfway across the dimly lit room, Tim was on a ladder hanging up a very real-looking skeleton. Nicole stood on the floor next to him, babbling like a maniac.

"See, in *The Wizard of Oz*, Dorothy was from Kansas, and I'm from Kansas, so this could not be a more perfect costume for me, don't you think?" she blathered.

Tim gave her a "what is your problem" look. "Okay," he agreed reluctantly.

Nicole nodded excitedly. Tim was so adorable, and so far they were getting along great! Who knew that Dorothy and a mummy could be a match made in heaven? "Yeah." Nicole tapped her finger on her forehead, trying to think of something else to talk about. "So . . . what's your favorite vegetable? I like corn. You a corn guy, Tim?" she asked, looking up at him adoringly. But suddenly Zoey was at her side, tugging on her elbow. Nicole looked at her, a little annoyed. What did she want? Couldn't her roommate see she was busy?

"'Scuze us just a sec," Zoey said to Tim as she pulled Nicole aside.

"What?" Nicole said, annoyed. What was so important that she had to interrupt the scintillating conversation she was having with the most adorable mummy on the planet? She gave Tim a friendly wave to let him know she'd be back.

Zoey gave her friend a hard look. "I think you're coming on a little too strong," she said, holding up her fingers for emphasis. If Nicole didn't back off a little, Tim would probably think she was a stalker.

Frowning, Nicole turned back to gaze at her dream guy. "But I have to marry him," she confided to Zoey.

The pleading look in her eyes let Zoey know Nicole was serious about this boy. But that didn't mean that she couldn't give her some good — and essential — advice. She was serious about every boy. "Okay, but you just need to —"

"Blaaaaahhhh!" came a loud voice behind them. Zoey turned around to see Chase dressed in a tuxedo with a red-lined black cape. His naturally curly hair was slicked back smoothly. He made a fierce magician. But what was with the black lipstick?

"Oh, hey, Chase," Zoey said.

"Hi, Chase." Nicole waved.

Chase looked puzzled. "What, you weren't scared?" he asked.

Zoey shrugged and exchanged glances with Nicole. "Why would we be scared of a magician?" she asked.

Chase scowled. What magician? He looked down at his black cape. . . . "No, no, no, no." They had it all wrong. "I'm a vampire," he explained just as Logan appeared from inside the Tunnel of Doom. He smiled when he saw Chase. "Hey, Mister Magic . . ." he greeted.

Magician! Magic? These guys didn't get it. "I am a vampire!" he practically shouted. "Do you guys wanna see the receipt for my costume?" He started searching his pockets in frustration.

Logan waved a hand dismissively. He didn't have time to discuss costumes — he had to get the haunted house finished!

"Whatever," he said. "I need you and your little girlfriends to come gimme a hand in the Tunnel of Doom." He shook the skull he was holding in their direction before turning back to the tunnel.

Zoey straightened. It was time to get to work. "C'mon, let's go help him. You can do a magic trick for me later," she told Chase, unable to resist getting a jab in.

Chase watched the girls disappear into the tunnel. "I am not a magici —" He stopped himself for a second, thinking, then held up his hands like Dracula. "Blaaahhh!" he said to himself. Ugh. Maybe they were right. Maybe his costume needed work. He didn't sound at all scary. He sounded lame. Totally frustrated, he followed the girls into the Tunnel of Doom.

*　　　*　　　*

At the other end of the haunted house, Quinn strolled past boxes and spooky props, whistling approvingly. She was already in her own costume — a perfect re-creation of Albert Einstein, if she did say so herself. Her bushy silver wig and mustache, bow tie, white lab coat, and glasses were all it took to transform her into the genius scientist she so admired. "Hey, cool haunted house," she murmured to her boyfriend, Mark Del Figgalo.

"Yeah," Mark said, nodding in agreement as he checked everything out. His mummy costume was actually bugging him a little — some of it was wrapped too tight. And Quinn hadn't even bandaged up his face yet.

Quinn surveyed her surroundings. "It's looking really scary —" When she spotted Tim in his mummy costume, Quinn stopped in her tracks. What was he doing dressed as a mummy? "Hey, you," she said bluntly as she stepped closer. "What's your name?"

Tim looked up from the casket he was preparing. "I'm Tim," he said casually.

Quinn thrust her hand out and gave this "Tim" a once-over. "Well, Tim, you should not be in a mummy costume," she announced.

"Why not?" Tim asked, looking at the girl Einstein like she was a mad scientist instead of a brilliant one.

Quinn glared. Was he serious? It was obvious.

"Because Mark is dressed like a mummy," she informed him.

Tim shrugged. "Who's Mark?"

"I'm Mark," Mark mumbled from behind Quinn.

"Why did you choose a mummy costume when you knew Mark was going to be a mummy?" Quinn asked accusingly.

Tim shook his head. What was with this girl? "How could I have known?" he asked pointedly.

"I wrote about it on my blog," Quinn replied. Duh. The whole campus read her blog daily, of course. "Now, go change," she ordered.

"Why should I go change —"

Quinn cut him off — she would not stand for an argument. "Go," she hissed.

"All right," he said, throwing up his hands. "Man." He grabbed the ladder next to him and walked off in a huff.

"I'm really sorry about this, man," Mark said softly as Tim passed by him. Mark had learned long ago it was best not to argue with Quinn.

"Whatever," Tim replied grumpily.

Quinn watched him go, satisfied that she had solved the problem in a manner worthy of her genius outfit. "Now, let's get your head bandages on," she told

Mark, leading him over to a large chair with several skulls hanging above it. "Sit."

"All right," Mark muttered, sitting down while Quinn unzipped her large scientist's bag and began to pull out mummy bandages.

On the other side of campus, Michael was walking up a short flight of stairs, talking on his phone. Dressed as a zombie, his unruly gray wig, tattered clothes, and pale makeup made him look a fright.

"Well, why do I have to wait for it?" he asked into his phone. He was tired of doing Logan's dirty work. He wanted to be working on the haunted house, not sitting around waiting for some truck to arrive. "But how come . . . just tell me why . . ." Logan was being his usual bossy self and wasn't budging to boot. It would probably be easier to just do what he wanted and get off the phone. "Fine, I'll do it. Bye," Michael said, snapping his phone shut. But he didn't stop talking. He was too steamed. "Logan . . . always ordering me around," he mumbled to himself. "And —"

Oof! Michael rounded a corner and ran right into Dustin.

"AHHHHHHH!" Dustin screamed at the sight of the ratty zombie.

"AHHHHHHH!" Michael screamed, too, looking around frantically to see what had scared Dustin and tripping over his own feet. A second later he was lying on the grass, still screaming.

Dustin stared at the writhing creature on the ground. He looked really familiar. . . .

"Michael?" he asked.

Michael stared up at Zoey's little brother. "Yeah, it's me," Michael said. His heart was thudding like crazy. "Why'd you scream like that, giving me a heart attack?"

"Sorry," Dustin said, still breathing a little hard himself. He reached out a hand and helped Michael to his feet. "Sorry," he said again sheepishly. "But you look really scary."

Proudly Michael adjusted his torn blue jacket. "Thanks," he said. "Now, you better go get your costume on, man. The haunted house starts as soon as it gets dark."

Dustin looked up at Michael's zombie getup. It really was awesome. "Yeah, I know. But shouldn't you be there setting up?" he asked.

Michael shook his head, irritated. "No, Logan's making me wait for some delivery truck bringing more stuff."

Dustin nodded. "Oh, well, sorry I almost gave you a heart attack," he said.

Half smiling, Michael put a hand to his jacket lapel. "It's cool. It's just my heart," he added sarcastically.

He pounded his chest lightly as Dustin hurried off. "There, it's going again," he joked, relieved that his heartbeat had returned to normal.

4
Sticky Situation

Back inside the haunted house, Quinn was wrapping Mark's head with mummy bandages. She had already covered his forehead, eyes, and nose. Only the mouth was left. "Okay, close your mouth," she instructed.

Mark pressed his lips together tightly and Quinn wrapped the bandages across his mouth so that his head was completely wrapped. Then she sealed everything off with a special mummy glue she had invented herself.

"'Kay. Now I'm using a powerful superadhesive glue so these bandages can't come off," she explained to Mark as she applied a generous amount of the stuff. "There. Done." She stepped back to admire her work.

"Mmnnnnhhhhmm." From inside the ancient-looking bandages, Mark mumbled something incoherent.

Quinn smiled. "Oooh, that's good. You sound just

like a mummy," she congratulated him while she rubbed her sticky hands together. "Uh-oh, I got some glue on my fingers. I better go get some solvent. Back in a sec." She grabbed her bag and headed out the door.

"Mmnnnnnnnhmm!!" Mark mumbled more loudly. He couldn't see anything, and his lips had been glued together! But Quinn was already gone.

Getting awkwardly to his feet, Mark reached his hands out in front of him to try and feel where he was going. But no matter how careful he tried to be, he kept bumping into stuff. Then, he heard voices. . . .

"Man . . . it's hot in there," Zoey said.

Nicole nodded. "Yeah, and scary. I think Logan's taking this haunted house thing way too seriously," she said gravely. But the moment Nicole spotted mummified Mark over by the coffin, the spooky tunnel was nothing but a distant memory. "Oooh, there's Tim," she breathed, her heartbeat accelerating.

"Oh, yeah," Zoey confirmed. "He finished putting on his mummy bandages."

Batting her eyes, Nicole gazed at her mummy adoringly. "How cute is that," she whispered. "Hi, Tim!" she called out.

"Mnnmmmhhhmmnnn," the mummy replied, waving his arms a little frantically and pointing to his mouth.

Nicole peered at him curiously. What was he trying to say? "What?" she asked.

Frustrated, Mark gave her a "forget it" gesture and turned to leave, stumbling over a tombstone.

Zoey watched him leave. "Where's he going?" she asked aloud. He wasn't going to get very far with his face all bandaged up.

Nicole felt a little shiver of excitement. "I dunno. Why don't I go find out?" she asked, hurrying after him. "Wish me luck!" she called back.

"Luck," Zoey said, smiling. She'd probably need it.

Michael stood on the sidewalk by the main entrance to PCA, looking at his watch impatiently. "Man, where is the stupid delivery truck?" he said aloud into the darkness. He was stuck here waiting while the haunted house construction went on without him. Shaking his head, he sat down on a bench next to the driveway. He looked around one more time for the truck, then lay back on the bench. If he had to wait here, he might as well get some relaxation in. Michael closed his eyes. Man, he was tired.

The next thing he knew, the visiting French boarding school teachers, Monique and Andre Jambon, were standing over him, looking panicked and talking in rapid-fire French.

"Oh, non, oh, non!" Andre cried.

"Regarder le garçon pauvre!" Monique added. *"Il a été dans quelque genre d'accident!"*

In spite of his French classes, Michael couldn't understand a word they were saying, but he sat up and smiled. He could be polite, at least. "Oh, hi," he greeted. "What's up?"

Andre looked totally thrilled to see him sitting up and talking. *"Remercier la bonté! Il est toujours vivant!"* he cried, clapping his hands together.

Monique examined Michael's face. "Uhhh . . . uhhh . . . hospital! We take you!" she said in her fractured English.

Michael blinked. "Hospital?" he repeated. What was she talking about? Then it dawned on him. They thought he needed medical attention! His zombie costume was so good, they thought he had been in some sort of accident. "Oh, no, no, no," he said, shaking his head. "I'm fine. I'm not hurt. This is just a costume. For Halloween." He said the last word slowly in case it would help them understand.

"Oui! Hospital!" Andre repeated, emphatically

27

grabbing Michael by the arm. Monique clutched his other arm and together they tried to move him toward the car.

Michael felt a wave of panic. "No, *Halloween*," he said again as Monique tightened her grip on his arm. "I'm not hurt. Lady, if I was hurt, why would you be grabbing me like that?" But Andre and Monique were not getting it, or letting go. Michael had to take action. "Help!" he shouted, trying to shake the French people off. "Help!"

Andre shouted back, "Yes! We help!"

Michael shook his head. "No!" he screamed, breaking free. They were not helping him at all. They were the problem! He took off running and didn't look back.

"Revenir!" Andre's voice called after him. Michael glanced over his shoulder and groaned. Monique and Andre were following him!

Nicole was following what she thought was her mummy. She chased the mute and mummified Mark down a long pathway and up a short flight of stairs next to a steep hill covered in vines, crying out to him to stop. "Tim! Hey! Here I am!" she called out cheerfully. Why wasn't he turning around? Taking matters into her own hands, Nicole rushed up to him, grabbed him by the shoulders, and turned him around. "Tim! I've been chasing you for, like, half an hour, yelling your name. You didn't hear me?" she asked.

"Hmmmnmmhhmmm," the mummy mumbled, gesturing wildly to his mouth.

Nicole smiled coyly. "What?" she asked, leaning in. "Is there something you want to ask me?"

"Huh?" The mummy shook his head, still mumbling. As Nicole got closer, he stepped backward. . . . She didn't understand. He had to get away. He took another step back and . . .

Suddenly the wrapped guy lost his footing and fell head over heels down the steep hill.

With a gasp Nicole watched her darling mummy tumbling quickly away from her. She watched him roll and roll, hitting the ground over and over on his way down the incline, until at last he landed on the sidewalk below. "Are you all right?!" she called, grimacing. That fall didn't look so good.

The mummy looked up at her. "Mnnhnnnmm."

"Okay, wait there!" Nicole instructed. "I'll find a way to get down there and help you!" Nicole turned down the path that led to the sidewalk below.

Aching, Mark pulled himself to his feet and staggered away, groaning incomprehensibly beneath his bandages.

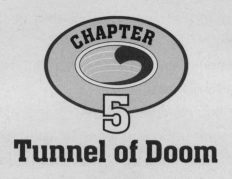

Tunnel of Doom

In the science building basement, the haunted house was finally finished and ready for visitors. The light was dim and eerie. The sound of howling wolves echoed in the basement chamber. Dustin, Jack, and five other underclassmen stood in line shivering and waiting to enter the Tunnel of Doom.

Smugly Logan eyed the line of kids from under his grim reaper hood. They were about to be terrified. "And now your nightmare begins," he said in a spooky voice, raising his scythe dramatically. "You are about to enter the most evil place on Earth —"

"Blaaaaaaaaaaahhhh!" Chase shouted, spreading his cape wide and leaping in front of the kids in his best vampire imitation.

Dustin, Jack, and all the kids stared at him.

"Hey, Chase," Dustin said, looking up at him from under his cowboy hat.

"Hey," policeman Jack added, looking bored.

Logan scowled at Chase. "Dude, you're ruining my haunted house," he stated.

Chase shook his head. "I'm scaring the children," he corrected. Only none of them looked scared.

"Hey, Chase. You a magician?" Dustin asked after looking him over.

Chase scowled. "No! I'm a vampire!" he said hotly. Why did everyone keep calling him a magician? He had a pointed hairline, black lips, trickling blood, and fangs! Couldn't they see that?

"Zoey, please make him be quiet," Logan begged.

Zoey stepped forward and took Chase by the arm. "Come with me," she said gently, pulling him aside.

Chase looked at Zoey pleadingly. "You think I'm a vampire, right?" he asked.

Only sorta, Zoey thought. But she couldn't tell Chase that. "Yes. You're very scary," she told him reassuringly.

Those were the words Chase had been waiting to hear. "I know," he said, smiling to himself and shrugging modestly.

With the "magic man" out of the way, Logan turned

back to the waiting Halloweeners. "And now . . . if you dare, walk this way into the Tunnel of Doom!" He nodded to a kid over by the controls, who hit a switch. Lightning flashed, thunder boomed, and an evil-sounding laugh filled the air.

Dustin shivered. "Ummm . . . is there someplace else we could enter?" he asked nervously.

Logan smirked. "Why?" he asked, taunting the poor kid. "Scared?"

Dustin turned to look back at Jack, who was shaking so hard, his holster was jiggling. The other kids looked terrified, too. But they weren't about to admit it to Logan.

"No," Dustin insisted.

Logan nodded. "Good. This way, then." He gestured toward the gaping black mouth of the Tunnel of Doom.

The kids exchanged nervous looks as they stepped forward, making their way into the darkness.

With her hand on her hip, Zoey gave Logan a look. "Don't you scare them too much," she advised.

"Relax." Logan smirked and nodded knowingly. The fun was just beginning.

Inside the tunnel, it was dark and foggy. Red and blue lights flashed on and off as Dustin, Jack, and the other five kids moved farther in. Overhead lightning flashed, illuminating the giant spiderwebs, skeletons, zombies, and ghouls that hung at twisted angles on the walls.

Dustin looked around at the creepy stuff while the eerie sounds exploded in his ears. "Okay, this is a little scary," he admitted, trying to stay calm.

And then, out of nowhere, a low, whispering voice called a familiar name into the darkness, echoing over and over, "Jack, Jack, Jack, Jack, Jack, Jack."

Jack's eyes widened. "Okay, that's a *lot* scary. Why's that creepy voice saying my name?"

"It's just Logan messing with you," Dustin replied, waving a hand in the air and hoping it was true.

Ka-boom! An earsplitting crack of thunder ripped through the air. The lights went out, and an inhuman howl filled the tunnel. "Jack!" it wailed.

Dustin shivered. "Let's get outta here!!!" he shouted.

Screaming like banshees, the kids all raced out of the tunnel as quickly as they could.

Standing at the entrance, Zoey watched them stream past her, their eyes wide with fear. The poor little kids were freaked. Enough was enough.

"Are you trying to scare them all to death?!" she asked Logan accusingly.

Logan shrugged. "Yeah, pretty much," he admitted.

Zoey glared. "Turn on the lights right now!" she called to the kid working the controls.

"No!" Logan objected.

Zoey stood firm. "Yes!"

A second later the lights came on. Zoey turned around to see Dustin looking up at her, his expression full of terror.

"Zoey!" he cried.

Smiling at her little brother, Zoey tried to reassure him that everything was fine. "Aw, Dustin, it's okay."

"No!" Dustin insisted. "I can't find Jack!"

Zoey's eyebrows furrowed. "What do you mean?"

"He was right beside me a minute ago! Where'd he go?!" Dustin cried.

Turning to the grim reaper, Zoey demanded an explanation. "Logan?" she said accusingly.

Logan looked nonplussed. "He's probably still in the tunnel," he said, shrugging it off.

But just then Chase emerged from the tunnel shaking his head. "No, he's not. Tunnel's empty," he confirmed.

Zoey glared at Logan, her arms folded tightly

across her white satin dress, waiting for him to explain what had happened.

Logan raised his red-gloved reaper hands defensively. "I didn't do anything to the kid!" he insisted.

"Then where is he?" Zoey asked, looking around. Jack was definitely missing.

Thunder boomed, and evil laughter filled the air once more. This was not good.

CHAPTER 6

Disappearing Act

The little kids huddled in the corner of the creepy basement, sticking close together while Chase, Logan, and Zoey searched for Jack.

"Jack!" Chase spun around quickly, looking in all directions. His cape swirled out behind him.

"Hey, Jack?" Zoey called into the dark corners of the basement.

"Jack?" Logan yelled. He actually sounded a little worried. But maybe he was just frustrated that Jack didn't answer when he called . . . or reappear. "Where is that kid?" Logan asked, clutching his long-handled blade. Jack couldn't have disappeared into thin air.

Chase held out his hands, palms down. "I dunno, but this is getting a little weird," he confessed.

"A little weird?" Zoey looked at Chase like he was completely buggin'. He had just made the understatement of the century. "Dustin's roommate is missing. That's worse than a little weird," she pointed out.

Dustin did not want to just stand around listening to the big kids argue about how weird the situation was — he wanted to take action. "I'm going to look in the tunnel!" he told them.

"He's not in there," Chase insisted. He had checked it out himself.

"Well, that's the last place he was, and somebody's gotta find him!" Dustin shouted. The panic in his voice was plain.

"Dustin, come back here," Zoey yelled after her brother, but he was already gone. Zoey started to go after him but Chase stopped her.

"Just let him look," he said quietly, opening his arms and cape. "It can't hurt." Chase figured the poor kid needed something to do.

"Well, I don't want him to disappear, too!" Zoey said, sounding almost as upset as her brother.

"Look, there's no way a little kid could just 'disappear' in that tunnel," Chase explained calmly.

"Unless someone made him disappear." The accusing tone was back in Zoey's voice. She whirled around to glare at Logan, the skirt of her white Marilyn Monroe dress swishing around her legs. The other kids turned their eyes on Logan, too. Even Chase was staring at him . . . hard.

Logan looked back at all of the accusing eyes. "What?" He held out his hands and shrugged. This was not his fault.

Chase pointed a finger at his least favorite roommate. "Is this your idea of a funny prank?" he asked. "'Cause if it is, you're taking it way too far!"

"Oh, come on!" Logan could not believe they thought he had something to do with this!

"You come on," Zoey shot back. This was exactly the kind of prank Logan would pull.

"Where's Jack?" Chase demanded.

"I don't know!" Logan insisted.

Chase narrowed his black-lined eyes. He looked at Zoey. "He's lying."

"Totally lying," Zoey agreed.

"Look, if I'm lying, then . . . then . . ." Logan stammered, pointing his shiny red glove at his two friends, struggling to come up with *something* to convince them that he was telling the truth.

"Then what?" Zoey tapped her foot and waited. This had better be good.

"Then . . ." Finally Logan had it. "Then I hope I

wake up tomorrow *not* great-looking," he said, waving his hands for emphasis. It was the worst thing he could possibly imagine.

Zoey and Chase exchanged a look. It was positive proof.

"He's telling the truth." Chase nodded.

"Totally telling the truth," Zoey agreed. Logan's looks were his most prized possession. There was no way he would ever wish to be ugly, or even just 'regular' good-looking. After all, he was his own number one admirer.

But it left them back at square one. Jack was still gone and Logan wasn't responsible for his disappearance.

Suddenly a noise made everyone turn. Slowly Dustin emerged from the tunnel. He was walking with his arms outstretched, a strange lumpy object balanced upon them. Lights flashed behind him and the eerie laugh echoed from inside the tunnel.

"Dustin, what is that?" Zoey looked from the small lifeless object in his arms to the totally stunned look on her younger brother's face. He seemed completely shell-shocked. "Dustin?" she repeated, speaking gently. "What are you holding?"

The wiry blond kid was barely able to speak. "It's . . . it's the hat Jack was wearing," he stammered, offering up the police hat.

Zoey looked at Logan. Logan looked at Chase. Chase looked at Zoey. All of them looked scared. In the corner the little kids picked up on their fear and cowered closer together as the voice from inside the tunnel began to snarl. Zoey took Jack's hat from Dustin's arms and stared at it. It was not a good sign. Things were getting spookier by the second. . . .

I Want My Mummy!

Professor Albert Quinstein ran down one of the large outdoor stairways on the PCA campus. Her crazy white hair and mustache glowed eerily in the moonlight as she hurried past other costumed students.

Quinn was frantic. Forget discovering the theory of relativity, all this scientist wanted to discover was where her mummy, Mark, was. She had the solution they needed to loosen Mark's facial bandages in her black medical bag, but now she was missing Mark.

"Mark? Mark . . . ?" Quinn called as she ran. "Have you seen a mummy?" she asked desperately, looking into the confused face of a hippie boy wearing a ring of flowers in his hair.

The flower child shrugged and shook his head. "Sorry."

"That's not helpful!" Quinn snapped before she hurried on. "Mark? Mark . . . ? Mark . . . ?

Meanwhile, Michael was still fleeing from the overly helpful French professors. And he was getting tired. He pulled himself around the corner of the PCA gym, wishing he could just collapse in a heap and never move again. He felt like he had been running for hours!

"I'm not injured!" he yelled, out of breath. It was useless. The teachers didn't understand what he was saying at all. "It's Halloween!" Michael sobbed, stumbling on. How long could he keep running? And how could he make two non-English speakers understand about Halloween?

The Jambon teachers were getting closer all the time. Their voices rang in Michael's ears.

"*arrêter de courir!*" Andre shouted, trying to get the boy to stop.

"*nous devons vous prendre à un hôpital!*" Monique added loudly.

"Aw, man." Unless he wanted to spend the night in the hospital, Michael had to keep on running.

"*S'il vous plait!*"

"*attentez!*"

The teachers chased after him, pleading desperately in French for him to stop and wait.

*　　*　　*

"Okay . . ." Chase turned to Logan. He was going to give him one more chance to explain the missing kid. "How could Jack have lost his hat?" he demanded, examining the police cap in his hands.

"I keep telling you — I don't know," Logan answered angrily. How many times did he have to explain that he was as baffled as they were?

"You designed this haunted house," Zoey pointed out. Logan was the one person who knew all the ins and outs. Even if he didn't make Jack disappear, he should have a good idea of where he might be.

"So where's Jack?" Dustin cried frantically.

"Look . . ." Logan held up his hands. "I promise you, we'll find —"

Suddenly the basement lights went out — all of them. The already nervous kids were plunged into darkness.

Everyone screamed.

"What happened to the lights?" Logan yelled.

"The power went out!" Zoey said, trying to keep her voice calm. She didn't want to freak the younger kids out any more than they already were.

"I'm scared!" Zoey heard Dustin beside her. She reached a hand toward him.

"Just wait, wait, wait . . ." Chase was fumbling with something. Zoey could hear him rustling around and then . . .

"It's okay." Chase breathed a small sigh of relief as he found the switch he was looking for and turned on a small battery-powered lantern. The light coming from it was pretty weak, but it was enough to dimly illuminate the large room.

"Did you shut off the power?!" Zoey accused Logan.

"No!" Logan insisted. Why was she blaming him for everything? He was innocent!

"He couldn't have," Chase confirmed. "He was standing right next to me." And the power switch was against the wall.

Even if Logan hadn't cut the power, Zoey'd had enough. "Okay, you know what? A kid is missing, the power's out . . . I'm going to get Dean Rivers," she said, heading for the door.

"I'm on board with that," Chase said as he followed her.

Zoey pushed the bar across the door to release the latch and open it. Nothing happened. She tried it again. Nothing.

"It's locked," she said, turning back to the group.

"What do you mean?" Logan demanded.

"What do you mean, what do I mean?" Zoey asked, feeling exasperated. She was talking fast and getting madder by the minute. "I said the door's locked! How many definitions of 'locked' are there?"

Chase stepped in to keep the peace — the last thing they needed was a fight. "Okay, calm down," he said gently.

Suddenly the video screen hanging high up in the corner of the basement came on and a tortured voice cried out.

"Look," Dustin shouted, pointing to the flickering fuzzy image on the screen. It was Jack! He was standing in some sort of fog, reaching out with both arms and calling to them.

"Help meeeee . . . help meeee . . ." Jack cried in an echoey voice.

"It's Jack!" Logan could not believe his eyes.

"Dude, where are you?!" Dustin called. But his friend didn't answer. He peered out from the screen blankly. Then, suddenly, his face twisted in pain and he screamed.

Dustin answered his roommate's scream with one of his own and soon the entire basement of kids was shrieking again.

As quickly as he'd appeared, Jack disappeared from the screen and the crowd was left in the dim light of Chase's lantern and the glowing screen.

Dustin wrapped his arms around Zoey. The poor kid was completely freaked out, and so were his friends. "What's happening?" Dustin cried.

It was a good question.

Michael ran into the lounge of the girls' dorm and stopped to catch his breath. The lounge was deserted — for the moment. Michael knew it would not be long before the French teachers caught up with him again. They were relentless. He paused and listened hard for the sound of footsteps or shouting.

Everything was silent. "Lost 'em. Good!" Michael said quietly to himself. Breathing a sigh of relief, he spotted the girls' Blix machine. A drink was just what he needed after his long hard run!

Michael took a cup from the dispenser, filled it with ice, and helped himself, muttering about his ridiculous predicament. "Crazy French people," he grumbled, shaking his head. He'd only had one sip of icy-cold Blix when he heard a noise that made his blood run even colder — more French! The visiting teachers were still after him!

"Où le jeune homme est allé?"

"Aw, man!" Ditching his drink, Michael looked around for a place to hide. The pickings were slim and time was short. The voices were getting closer! Without a second to spare, Michael dove behind the biggest couch in the lounge.

"Où est le garçon blessé?" Andre demanded to know where the injured boy was.

"Je ne sais pas! Regarder partout?" Monique had no idea, but they began to search the room.

From his hiding place behind the couch, Michael peeked out, watching his pursuers. The tall man, who was probably as thirsty as Michael was after their big chase, picked up Michael's abandoned cup and drank the rest of the contents. "Mmmm." He nodded approvingly.

Monique glared at Andre. Her expression said it all. What did he think he was doing? This was no time to enjoy a beverage. They were in the middle of an urgent search!

Andre motioned toward the soda machine. "Le Blix," he explained with a shrug. It was hard to resist.

Slapping the cup out of his hand, Monique gave Andre another steely look. This one said, "Quit wasting time and find that boy!" *"Chercher le garçon malade!"* she yelled in French in case her look left any doubt.

*   *   *

The power was still out in the haunted house, and tensions were running high. Zoey paced back and forth in the dim light coming from Chase's lantern and the inexplicably glowing TV screen. "We've gotta get outta here!" she cried, exasperated.

Chase agreed. But how? The doors were locked. "Why don't they have phones in basements?" he asked.

"We gotta find Jack!" Dustin reminded everyone that their first priority was really his missing roommate.

"Okay..." Zoey said, turning to her brother, "tell us the last thing that happened before he disappeared."

"Well...we were in that tunnel," Dustin said slowly, "and we heard someone calling his name...in a whisper, like 'Jack, Jack, Jack, Jack.'" Dustin imitated the spooky voice well. It made the hair on the back of Zoey's neck stand up.

"Well, who was calling his name?" Chase wanted to know.

"I dunno," Dustin said.

Logan started again slowly. Somewhere in the kid's explanation there had to be a clue. "Okay, so you were in the tunnel —"

Suddenly the lights began to flicker again like lightning and a deep voice echoed, "Dustin, Dustin, Dustin, Dustin . . ."

The kids looked in every direction, confused by the flashing lights. The voice seemed to be coming from everywhere at once. But they could not see anyone.

As the voice was replaced by a creepy evil laugh, Dustin grabbed Zoey and hung on for dear life. "Zoey, it's gonna get me!" he squealed.

"No, it's not!" Zoey tried to reassure him. She put her hands up to shield her eyes as the flashing lights grew more and more intense. They were blinding! And the noise! There was a loud crack like thunder and another flash.

Then, just like the flickering image of Jack, the lights and noise were gone.

Chase blinked to clear his vision. "Okay, that was freaky!" he said, in case anyone had missed it.

Even Logan looked spooked. "Yeah," he agreed.

Zoey looked around the darkened room — without the lightning flashes it was hard to see. She saw the kids still huddled in the corner. She saw Logan and Chase. But . . . "Wait, where's Dustin?" she shouted, her voice filled with panic.

"Aw, man!" Chase could not believe things were getting *worse*. "Dustin...?" he called into the murky room.

There was no answer.

"Dustin!!!" Zoey screamed.

CHAPTER 8

Unmasked

Behind the couch in the girls' lounge, Michael willed himself to look like a footstool. The crazy French teachers were still looking for him and getting closer by the second.

"*Où vous êtes?*" Andre called.

"*Garçon malade?*" Monique wanted to find the sick boy. Why didn't he answer her? "*Pouvez-vous nous entendre?*" She only wanted to help. If she could only locate the poor child . . .

Andre was not about to give up either. "*Nous voulons vous aider.*" He was going to help the kid whether he wanted it or not.

"Ah!" At last Andre spotted Michael behind the couch.

Michael cringed and groaned as the couple pulled him out of hiding. "No, no, I don't need to go to a hospital!" he protested. How could he make them understand?

Monique looked horrified by Michael's appearance. *"Vous nous êtes avec fourni!"*

"Vous devez voir un médecin!" Andre insisted.

"Okay, I don't know what you're saying, but you guys are really getting on my nerves." Michael's head rolled on his shoulders. He was just about at the end of his rope and did not have the strength to keep running anymore.

A loud angry groan filled the lounge, making Michael start and look around. *Was that me?*

Whatever it was, it changed Monique and Andre's tune . . . and fast!

Monique pointed to the door behind Michael, her eyes wide. *"Monstre! Monstre!"* she yelled.

The dude Andre was buggin' just as hard. *"Course! Rapidement! Avant qu'il mange nos cerveaux!"* he shouted as he dashed for the door.

Michael tried to shout an explanation to let them know that the "monster" that had just come into the lounge was just another kid in costume and that he had no interest in eating their brains. But then he realized this was his opportunity. At last Monique and Andre were running *away* from him.

Grateful, he turned to the mumbling mummy and put a hand on his bandage-wrapped shoulder. "I don't know who you are, but I love you and your costume," he exclaimed before grabbing the mummy in a big hug.

The mummy groaned.

"Tim!" Nicole rushed into the lounge out of breath. "There you are!" she exclaimed. The mummy groaned again and hung his head in defeat.

"I thought you were hurt," Nicole said, jutting out her lower lip in a pout. "Why do you keep running away from me?"

The mummy mumbled again. His grunts and groans sounded a lot like "I'm not Tim!" But nobody seemed to notice. Or care.

"'Sup, Tim. Later, Tim." Michael gave the guy a last grateful pat before waltzing toward the exit, finally free of his pursuers.

"Where ya goin'?" Nicole asked.

"Back to my room so I can throw my French book in the garbage," Michael said over his shoulder. He never wanted to hear "the language of love" again, ever.

Nicole shrugged. She kind of liked French — it sounded pretty. But that wasn't important right now. What was important was that she had finally caught up to her dream guy. They were together at last . . . with no one else around.

"So, Tim . . . looks like we're alone," Nicole said, bouncing on the balls of her feet and clasping her hands together.

"Huh?" the mummy mumbled.

Nicole grinned flirtatiously. "Uh-huh! Here, let's get this tape off your mouth." She reached up, grabbed one side of the bandages covering her mummy's mouth, and gave a tug. Nothing. She pulled harder. "Wow . . . it's really stuck on there." She yanked with all her might.

Just then Dr. Quinn, Genius Woman, came running into the lounge. "There you are!" she shouted.

Nicole rolled her eyes. Talk about bad timing. She was alone with her dream guy and didn't want company. "Quinn . . . not now," Nicole said in singsong, jerking her head toward her waiting beau. She was hoping Quinn would get the point and leave them alone.

Nicole's mummy seemed to agree. He mumbled more loudly and began to wave his arms. It was sweet the way he wanted to scare Einstein away!

Nicole kept on tugging. When Quinn bailed, she wanted to be ready.

"What were you doing?!" Quinn demanded.

"Trying to get the bandages off his mouth," Nicole said. Wasn't it obvious?

"You can't do that without a special solvent." Quinn shook her head and pushed Nicole out of the way. "Move," she told her. Then she took a small spray bottle out of her bag and misted over the mummy's face.

"There. Now . . ." Quinn peeled the bandages back and Mark's face emerged, gasping for air. His lips had been glued shut for what seemed like forever.

Nicole stared in horror. "M . . . Mark? MARK!" It was supposed to be Tim under all of those raggedy bandages, not Quinn's boyfriend, Mark!

Quinn didn't seem too happy to see Mark, either. "Where have you been for the past three hours?" She sounded really annoyed.

"Running away from her!" Mark said, jabbing a finger at Nicole.

Quinn looked from Mark to Nicole and back. "Why?" she asked.

"'Cause she was chasing me!" Mark explained.

As Quinn slowly turned around to face Nicole, Nicole raised her hands in surrender. The look on Quinn's face was frightening. Talk about a mad scientist!

"Okay, now wait a minute..." Nicole tried to explain.

"You were chasing after my sweetheart?" Quinn demanded, flinging her hand back toward Mark and catching him in the chest.

"Well, yeah," Nicole admitted, "but, see, I thought —" Nicole didn't have a chance to say any more.

"You are dead meat, woman!" Quinn shouted, showing her fist. It was all Nicole needed to see. She turned in her ruby slippers and ran screaming for the door.

"Come back here and face my wrath!" Quinn shouted like the Wicked Witch of the West as she barreled after the shrieking Dorothy.

Alone in the lounge, Mark shook his head, haunted by the night's events. "I hate Halloween," he grumbled.

Zoey sat on the edge of a coffin in the basement haunted house with her head in her hands.

"Zoey, c'mon, it's okay," Chase tried to console her, helping her to her feet.

"It's not okay! My little brother and his roommate are missing!" Zoey cried. She sounded totally hysterical.

And she wasn't the only one. Logan, the haunted house master himself, was pacing frantically back and forth and wringing his hands. "She's right, man. This is bad. This is, like, *bad* bad." Logan didn't even try to hide the fear in his voice.

A thunderclap stopped Logan in his tracks.

"Uh-oh. The lights."

The lightninglike flashes started again...and then...the voice! But it wasn't Dustin's name being called this time. Or even Jack's.

"Logan, Logan, Logan, Logan, Logan..." the echoey voice called.

Backing into a corner, Logan looked all around, panicked. He was next!

"Logan, Logan, Logan, Logan, Logan..." the creepy voice repeated.

"Leave me alone!" Logan shouted.

"Look out, man!" Chase cautioned. "Don't let it get you!"

"No way!" Logan shrieked. "I'm gettin' outta here!" He ran for the locked door and crashed into it, hard. The door didn't budge. Logan ran at it again and again while the lights flashed.

"Dude, the door's locked!" Chase yelled. It was hopeless.

Throwing himself at the second double door,

Logan finally broke out. "Help! Help! Someone help meeeeee!" he screamed as he raced down the dark hallway and out of the basement lab.

With Logan gone, the haunted house got very quiet.

"Well . . . he's gone," Chase said. A mysterious smile played on his black-stained lips.

"Good." Zoey grinned. "Turn on the lights."

Chase pulled a remote control out of his black cape and pushed a button. The lights came on and the crowd of kids in the corner cheered like they had just watched their team win the championships.

Zoey opened the coffin she had been sitting on a few minutes earlier so Dustin and Jack could climb out. Their Halloween trick was over, and boy, was it a treat!

"What happened?" Jack asked, smiling.

"Did he fall for it?" Dustin wanted to know.

"Totally!" Zoey nodded. She had never seen Logan look so scared. He really thought he was done for.

"I think he may have had a stroke." Chase shook his head, still smiling.

Dustin and Jack slapped hands with their accomplices. They had pulled it off! "That's what he gets for trying to scare us," Dustin said.

"He messed with the wrong dudes," Jack agreed gleefully.

"Yeah. Think he learned his lesson?" Dustin asked.

"I doubt it." Zoey and Chase both shook their heads. It was hard to pound anything through Logan's thick skull. He'd be back, and he'd cause trouble again. But at least he was gone for now.

"Well, c'mon!" Chase turned the music up and the lights down. "It's Halloween! Let's party it up!" And the motley crew boogied down in the haunted house without fear.

The Chase and Michael Show: Not Funny

A few days later, Halloween seemed like a distant dream. But Nicole (who never quite forgave her mummy Tim for turning out to be Mark) was in the middle of a new nightmare. And she was doing her best to bury it in popcorn.

Lola and Quinn spotted her on their way to class. Nicole was slumped at a table, stuffing her face with popcorn, surrounded by empty Blix and water bottles. In spite of the cute layered pink-and-green tank and T-shirt she was wearing, she looked utterly miserable.

"Nicole?" Lola called, stepping over to the bottle-strewn table. She wasn't even sure she recognized her roommate. Nicole never looked glum. Lola scrunched up her eyebrows under the turquoise spangled skullcap she had pulled over her long red-streaked hair. Lola liked her hat, along with her big hoop earrings and boundless beads. Lately she'd been going for a funky bohemian look. Nicole, it seemed, was going for more of a big-bucket-of-movie-popcorn wallowing thing.

"Hi," Nicole said sadly.

"What's wrong?" Quinn, who was dressed in her usual quirky style, tried not to look shocked. Nicole's irrepressible perkiness was completely buried in snack food!

Nicole took a big slug of water, set down the bottle, and pouted up at her friends. "Stuff," she said, trying hard not to cry.

Are those tears? Lola wondered. This was serious. She and Quinn sat down next to Nicole to hear more.

"What stuff?" Lola asked gently.

"I —" Nicole floundered for the right words. She looked up at the sky, as if the words might come to her like falling rain. "I . . . I think I may have gotten a D on my algebra test," she blurted at last.

Quinn planted her elbow on the table and rested her head on her fist. This wasn't making any sense. There had to be a reasonable explanation. "You're a straight-A student," she said calmly.

"Yeah, those were the days," Nicole said mournfully. Her academic career was over!

"All right, what happened?" Lola asked. They

would get to the bottom of this. And they would find a way out, too.

"Lance McAllister, Daniel James, and Harry Matthau. *That's* what happened." Nicole named the three cutest guys in her algebra class before shoving more popcorn in her mouth.

Lola turned to Quinn. "Are you following this?" she asked, confused. What did boys have to do with math?

"No," Quinn said, baffled. "And I have an IQ of 177."

The two girls looked back at Nicole, hoping she could throw them at least one more piece to the puzzle.

Nicole only threw up her hands. What was so hard to get? "You are not understanding the problem," she whined. "The three cutest guys in the ninth grade are sitting all around me and I'm supposed to concentrate on algebra?"

That explained it. Nicole was completely boy-crazy. But there was a quick fix. "Well, when you're in class, just focus on the work and forget about the cute guys," Quinn suggested rationally.

"Yeah, like that's possible." Nicole rolled her eyes. Did Quinn know her at all? Cute guys were her *life.*

"Well, you better figure out something, 'cause it's not gonna help to just drown your sorrows in popcorn and Blix," Lola said, helping herself to a handful of corn. It actually looked pretty good.

"Okay, you two give bad advice," Nicole complained as she shoveled in another handful. "Where's Zoey?" She needed to talk to somebody with some *good* ideas.

"Hanging out in the boys' dorm watching Chase and Michael do their Webcast," Quinn answered with her mouth full.

"Webcast?" This was the first Lola had heard about a Webcast. She looked at Quinn, waiting for further explanation.

Quinn shrugged. "It's just this little comedy show they do together that people can watch online."

"What kind of comedy?" Lola asked. Sure, she knew Michael and Chase could be funny . . . but a whole show?

Michael smiled into the tiny Webcam mounted to his computer monitor, checking to see that the graphics they had created were coming up on the screen. Sure enough, THE CHASE & MICHAEL SHOW appeared across the guys' chests in small blue letters. With the touch of a button, the graphics faded away and Michael began to introduce the next segment, "And right now . . ."

"Here on *The Chase and Michael Show*," Chase completed Michael's sentence.

Then Michael gestured back toward Chase. "My boy Chase will gargle the national anthem with coffee."

Chase gestured back toward Michael. "While Michael trims his nose hairs with a *professional* nose-hair trimmer." He emphasized the word *professional* so people would know this was not just something they came up with off the cuff. They had planned this.

"And . . ." Michael prompted, ready with his trimming device. Chase held up his big coffee mug.

"We begin." Chase took a giant swig of coffee. Michael turned on the trimmers and started on nostril number one.

From a bright yellow beanbag chair off-camera, Zoey watched everything while she highlighted passages in one of her textbooks. It was hard to say what was worse — the faces Michael was making as he lost nasal hair or the noises escaping Chase's coffee-filled throat. It was all pretty repulsive and, honestly, Zoey wasn't sure that the whole *Chase and Michael Show* was gonna fly. But at least it was making her English homework more entertaining.

Then, just as Chase got to the part in the national anthem about "the dawn's early light," his gargling sputtered, stopped, and turned into a horrible choking cough. He sounded awful, like he was going to expire right there on the spot.

Panicked, Michael dropped his trimmers and began whacking Chase on the back and grabbing him around the throat in a way that did not look helpful. Zoey wasn't sure if she should step in or not. Chase really sounded bad.

Right behind Zoey's beanbag, lounging on his bed, Logan watched the scene with a vaguely amused expression, followed by a roll of his eyes.

"Uh, uh, okay." Michael kept pounding on Chase while he nervously talked to the still live camera. "I wanna make sure my buddy Chase here doesn't choke to death. Please enjoy this fine cartoon featuring us . . . in toon form." Michael punched a few keys on the PC and tiny animated Chase and Michael toons began hopping up and down on the screen, singing.

"I'm Chase."

"I'm Michael."

"We're hopping."

"We're hopping."

While the toons sang, the real Michael turned to his friend. "You all right, man?" he asked as soon as the camera was off.

"Yeah," Chase replied, gasping for air. "Just a little coffee in my lungs. No biggie," he said. When he could breathe normally again, he turned to Logan and Zoey. "So, uh, how do you like the show so far?"

"It's funny," Zoey said with an encouraging smile.

Logan propped himself up on one elbow. "It could not be worse," he enunciated cruelly, staring Chase straight in the face. It was possible that Logan was still sore about being scared out of his own haunted house. It was possible that he was being his usual jerky self. And it was possible that he was speaking the truth.

In any case, it wasn't very nice. And Zoey'd had it with Logan's mean streak.

"Can you say one nice thing to someone once?" she asked hotly, shooting a look at Logan over her shoulder.

"Sure." Logan shrugged. "You look pretty hot in those jeans."

Zoey wrinkled her nose. "You're disgusting."

"Look," Logan tried to explain himself. "I'm just trying to give these guys some constructive criticism so they don't get trashed in the school paper . . . *again*."

"Huh?" Zoey looked at Chase for explanation. She didn't know what Logan was talking about.

"This reporter for the *Daily Stingray* reviews our show every week," Chase explained glumly.

"And every week he slams us," Michael said, shaking his head. He thought their show was pretty good, but according to the reporter, it was a total waste of time and bandwidth.

"Maybe that's why only seven kids at PCA watch it," Logan said, like he was talking to a pair of preschoolers.

"Nine, thank you," Chase corrected, giving Logan the stink eye.

"Yeah!" Michael backed up his bud, then tapped Chase to let him know they were going on. "Come on, we're back." Michael pointed to the monitor. Chase hit a few keys on the keyboard and the jumping animated Chase and Michael gave way to the real deal.

"Okay, and we're back on *The Chase and Michael Show*," Chase announced.

"Which is lame!" taunted a voice offscreen.

"And that was the voice of our highly obnoxious roommate, Mister Logan Reese," Chase explained to the viewers with a sigh.

Michael shook his head. If Logan was gonna be a part of the show, maybe he should *really* be a part of the show. "Say hi to our viewers," Michael suggested, turning the little round Webcam and zooming in on Logan.

"Wow." Logan shrugged and looked right into the lens. "I've never said hi to nine losers all at once," he said snottily.

"Isn't he sweet?" Michael asked while wearily refocusing the Webcam on the show hosts.

"Now say hello to a special friend of *The Chase and Michael Show*." Chase thought it might be good to show a supportive watcher as well. Besides, Zoey looked really cute in her purple T-shirt with a round pin on her shoulder. Yeah, a cute, supportive watcher could help.

Zoey was not so sure. "N-n-n-n . . ." Zoey shook her head and held her hands up in protest. They better not be talking about her. She was not ready for a live broadcast. . . .

But it was too late.

Michael swung the little camera around again. "Say hi, Zoey," he prompted.

"Hi." Zoey smiled shyly and waved.

"So, Zoey, what should Chase and I talk about next?" Michael asked.

"I dunno. Movies?" Zoey suggested.

"Yeah," Logan piped up behind her. "Talk about how girls like stupid movies."

"Excuse me?" Zoey could not believe her ears.

Logan got up and walked behind Chase and Michael to get a drink and Zoey followed. Logan couldn't say something like that and just walk away.

Chase decided to ignore the fight breaking out behind him. "So, Michael, what kinds of movies do you like?"

"Well, Chase, I mostly go for —" Michael tried to ignore the fight, too, but it was impossible. He stopped talking midsentence. Nobody would have heard his answer over Zoey's angry voice, anyway. When that girl was mad, she was all business.

"What do you mean, girls like stupid movies?" Zoey demanded.

"I think you know what I mean," Logan replied casually.

"Why don't you take this outside?" Michael motioned toward the computer, hoping Logan and Zoey would take the hint. Hello. They were kinda ruining the show. . . .

Zoey didn't even notice. She wanted to hear what Logan thought was so stupid about the movies girls liked. "Tell me, Logan," she demanded.

"All girls want to see are dumb, sappy love stories," Logan replied.

"So?" Zoey retorted. "All guys want to see is stuff getting blown up."

"Trying to do a show here," Michael tried again to get Logan and Zoey's attention. It was useless.

Logan smiled, thinking of things blowing up. "That's better than romantic chick flicks," he argued.

"I'd rather see a romantic chick flick than a dumb car chase," Zoey countered.

"You don't even know what you're talking about." Logan tried to blow Zoey off.

No how. No way. "I know exactly what I'm talking about." Zoey crossed her arms and really laid into Logan. "You are the worst!"

The two of them got louder and louder, talking over each other while Chase and Michael quietly began to thumb wrestle. So much for *The Chase and Michael Show*!

The Great Debate

The next day at lunch, Logan, Chase, and Michael sat soaking up the sun at a big round table with trays of food. Logan leaned back in his chair so everyone could read his sleeveless T-shirt — which read WORST — Something Zoey had called him only the day before. He eyed Chase's dessert.

"Hey, you gonna eat that cookie?" he asked casually.

Chase picked up his chocolate chip cookie and whipped it across the table. It bounced off Logan's tray and landed in his lap.

"Was that necessary?" Logan asked, plucking crumbs from his attire.

"Yes," Chase grumped. He was still totally bent from the day before.

And so was Michael. "You ruined our show," he pointed out.

"Zoey started it," Logan accused.

"No," Zoey replied, walking up with a tray of salad, grapes, and bottled water. "*You* started it." She stared hard at Logan.

"You both ruined it." Michael smiled and spread his arms out like he was bestowing a generous gift. "How about that?" Maybe he had finally found something they could agree on.

Chase, for one, definitely agreed that Logan and Zoey had ruined it. "Which is why, from now on, when we do our show *you* can't be in the room." He pointed a finger at Logan.

Logan leaned forward in his seat. There was just one obvious piece of information Chase seemed to be ignoring. "I live there," he stated.

"Yes," Chase agreed. "But together Michael and I can overpower you." To demonstrate their team power, Michael and Chase butted their fists together and smiled.

"So, you're out," Michael concluded.

"Ha-ha," Zoey mocked Logan, making her high blond bun bounce on top of her head. She loved to see Logan lose.

"You too, Zoey," Michael added.

"What?" Zoey was not hearing this.

"Dude?" Chase looked at Michael. As far as Chase was concerned, Zoey was not the problem. She was welcome — no matter what.

"She can't come over while we're doing the show, either. She's banned!" Michael insisted. "For life," he added to show that he was serious.

"Aw, c'mon!" Chase whined. Michael was carrying this a little too far.

"It's fine," Zoey gave in. "I promise not to come over and ruin your little show again," she teased as she opened her bottle of water and took a sip.

"Hey." Lola walked up behind Chase and Michael wearing a turquoise-and-black-striped halter top and carrying the school paper. "You guys read today's *Stingray*?" she asked.

"No," Chase answered glumly. He could already imagine what it said after their last show-stopping broadcast.

"How bad did our show get trashed this time?" Michael asked, resigned.

"Check it out!" Lola handed the paper to Chase with a mysterious smile on her face and took a seat beside Zoey to drink her Blix.

"Okay . . ." Chase fumbled for the right page and

skimmed down to the good . . . or bad . . . part. "Da, da, da, da, da. . . . Here: 'The usually lame *Chase and Michael Show* was actually pretty good yesterday,'" he read aloud.

Michael and Chase slapped five. "Hey, he called us 'pretty good!'" Michael exclaimed.

"I heard me!" Chase said.

"Keep reading," Lola prompted them.

"The usual silly gags were replaced by a lively and spirited debate between Zoey Brooks and Logan Reese."

"Interesting." Logan sat with one arm slung over the back of his seat.

"What else does it say?" Zoey asked, leaning in to hear.

Chase and Michael both looked a bit baffled as Chase kept reading. "'The new addition of debates between Zoey and Logan make *The Chase and Michael Show* a must-see Webcast here at PCA."

"Hey, our show got its first good review!" Michael and Chase did some more five slapping. They were both grinning. So was Lola.

Zoey and Logan just looked at Chase and Michael with raised brows. *The Chase and Michael Show* just got its first good review, all right — because of Zoey and Logan.

"Too bad I'm not allowed in our room anymore while you're doing it," Logan said, sitting back in his chair.

"Yeah, and too bad I'm banned for life," Zoey seconded. Since the reporter seemed to like Zoey and Logan's addition the best, *The Chase and Michael Show* had just received its first and *last* good review.

"So, um . . ." Chase began to hem and haw. They had a couple of fences to mend. "Zoey . . ." he began.

"And Logan," Michael added with a winning smile.

"Please be in our show," Chase begged.

"Please?"

Later that afternoon, Nicole sat in her room, grabbing handfuls of popcorn from the huge bowl on her lap and piling them into her pouting mouth. "Man, if I don't figure out a way to stop being distracted by cute guys, I'm gonna flunk algebra and end up a hobo!" she complained to Quinn and Lola. She needed to come up with a plan. But what could possibly make her stop thinking about boys?

"Would you be open to hypnosis?" Lola asked, flopping across one of the beds in their dorm room.

"Ooh, hypnosis!" Quinn spun her chair away from the computer. She loved talking about experimental therapies!

"What do you mean?" Nicole asked. How could hypnosis help?

"Well," Lola explained, "once I was in this play and I had to cry, right? But I couldn't. So my acting coach used this hypnosis technique to help me cry whenever I wanted to."

"So you think you can hypnotize me to stop being distracted by cute guys?" Nicole asked. She was liking the sound of this.

"Mmm-hmmm." Lola nodded confidently.

"It's worth a shot," Quinn said.

Nicole looked totally game. Her eyes got a distant look, like she was imagining the possibilities. Lola took it as a "yes" and started plotting.

"Okay. Quinn and I will look up some hypnosis techniques online, and in a few days . . ." Lola paused. Nicole was looking a little *too* distant! "Stop thinking about cute guys!" Lola snapped.

"Sorry!" Nicole was brought crashing back to reality. But only for a moment. As soon as Lola and Quinn left to begin looking up solutions, Nicole grabbed another handful of popcorn and let her mind go where it always did — the land of gorgeous guys!

*   *   *

"Welcome back to *The Chase and Michael Show!*" Michael greeted viewers to their Webcast. The two hosts were leaning over the backs of the orange chairs they usually broadcast from. They were not going to be sitting in them today. They had something else in mind.

"And now," Chase began the introduction, "for your enjoyment, we present a new ultracool regular feature on the show. Which we call . . ."

"'He Says, She Says,' with Zoey Brooks and Logan Reese." Michael motioned toward their costars, who were standing off camera.

"Their topic tonight: Would a woman make a better president of the United States than a man?" Chase posed the question. Then he and Michael bowed out and Logan and Zoey came in from the sides, took their seats, and got down to it.

"Absolutely not," Logan pronounced immediately. He slouched down in his chair and crossed his arms, dismissing the whole idea.

"You're an idiot." Zoey shook her head in disgust. This was not a debate, it was a debacle. She was glad she was wearing her T-shirt printed with pink-and-black skulls, because this was going to be Logan's funeral.

* * *

Back in Zoey's dorm, Lola and Nicole were logged on to watch the action.

"A woman *cannot* be president of the United States," Logan insisted.

"Name one reason," Zoey demanded. The least the jerk could do was attempt to back up his ridiculous statement.

"Because girls are too emotional. Every time she got a pimple she'd cry and then start a war with Switzerland." Logan shook his head at the horrible thought.

Fresh from the shower, Lola shook her towel-covered head, too. "That is the stupidest thing I have ever heard anyone say." Didn't Logan know Switzerland was neutral?

"Well, pimples do make me upset," Nicole pointed out. Lola looked hard at her roomie. "But I'm not gonna blow up Switzerland," Nicole said defensively.

In the lounge even more kids were tuning in to the Webcast. A huge crowd had gathered around a single tiny computer screen. "Quinn, hurry up and hook up your laptop so we can all see," a blond girl said anxiously.

"I'm hurrying! I'm hurrying!" Quinn was frantic.

She didn't want to miss anything, either — the debate was just getting juicy! "Stupid USB port!" Quinn cursed at the cable connection. "There!" she cried as she got the computer hooked up to the large-screen TV in the lounge at last.

Quinn sat down on the table in front of the TV and crossed her legs as everyone gathered around to watch Zoey toss a zinger back at Logan.

"Girls may be more emotional than guys, but we're way less violent," Zoey stated calmly.

"And your point is?" Logan sounded annoyed.

"That if a woman was president maybe we'd be less likely to go to war." Zoey hammered it home.

"What's wrong with war?" Logan threw his head back in his chair so he was looking at the ceiling. War was always cool in movies.

Zoey stared into the camera, totally stunned. Where should she begin?

Quinn stared at the screen feeling as exasperated as Zoey.

Then Michael dashed on-camera. "Okay, Logan, your closing argument," he prompted before dashing off.

"Guys make better leaders and everybody knows it," Logan stated, sounding utterly bored.

"Zoey, final thoughts," Chase said, quickly running on and off.

"A woman would make a better president, and Logan's a moron," Zoey said with a straight face.

Logan stared at Zoey. "Why don't you just admit that you're freakishly attracted to me?" he taunted.

"Okay, I admit it." Zoey smiled at Logan. "So, you wanna make out?"

Chase and Michael looked at each other. What was happening? A second ago their show was going great. Now suddenly it was spinning out of control. . . .

"Sure!" Logan smiled and leaned over in his chair.

"Good, pucker up," Zoey said sweetly. She leaned in . . . and blew a wet raspberry right in Logan's face before storming out of the boys' room.

"Agh!" Logan wiped spittle off of his face with his sleeve. "Hey," he yelled after Zoey, "this is not over!"

But the new feature was. Michael and Chase leaped into the orange chairs. "And that concludes this segment of 'He Says, She Says.'" Michael smiled like a newscaster.

"We'll be right back with more of the *The Chase and Michael Show*," Chase concluded before switching over to animation.

"Man, Zoey and Logan were fired up!" Michael sat back in his chair, still reeling from the debate.

"Yeah, man, they were off the hizzy," Chase agreed, trying a little street slang.

Michael squinted at Chase. *Hizzy?* What was the dude talking about?

"I'm sorry." Chase shrugged and looked down at his lap. Then something on the monitor caught his eye. "Hey, check out how many people are watching us online!"

"Two hundred sixty-four people?" Michael could barely believe it.

"Uh-huh." Chase nodded.

Michael was stoked. "We rock, dude!"

"Yep." Chase sat back, feeling satisfied. "I think these Zoey and Logan debates are gonna make the kids here at PCA really think, you know?"

"Yeah?" Michael was thoughtful for a moment. "They might really get people talking," he mused.

Canceled!

The kids in Mr. Bender's class were way past talking — they were yelling, all of them. Girls were shouting at boys. Boys were screaming back at girls. Nobody was in their seat and nobody was listening to Mr. Bender, who stood in the middle of the room begging them all to stop fighting.

"Hey, I am in charge here!" Bender insisted at the top of his lungs. No matter how loudly he yelled, he couldn't be heard above the din.

Unfortunately the din *could* be heard in the hall and had gotten the attention of Dean Rivers.

The dean strode into the classroom as Bender yelled for the third time, "Please take your seats!"

"Bender!" the dean summoned the English teacher with one word. Quickly Mr. Bender followed him back out of the classroom into the hallway.

"Dean Rivers." Mr. Bender nodded at his boss and waited a bit nervously to hear what he had to say.

"Having a little trouble controlling your class?" the dean asked accusingly. The dean's assistant stood with her arms crossed, looking at Mr. Bender like he was a kid in detention.

Bender knew he had some fast talking to do if he didn't want it to look like the *kids* were in charge of *him*. "The thing is, they got all whipped up about this debate they saw last night on a Webcast."

"Whose Webcast?" the dean demanded.

"Chase Matthews and Michael Barrett's," the teacher answered reluctantly. Chase and Michael were good students. The last thing Mr. Bender wanted to do was get them in trouble.

"How can a Webcast be so —"

"Dean Rivers! Dean Rivers!" Another teacher ran up to the dean, interrupting the conversation. "Some boys and girls are fighting down by the gym!" she said frantically.

"Fighting about what?" Dean Rivers wanted to know.

"Some Webcast they saw last night," the teacher panted.

Dean Rivers turned to his assistant. "You get

Chase Matthews and Michael Barrett in my office right now," he demanded.

"Yes, sir," his assistant answered before hurrying off to follow his orders.

"And you—" Dean Rivers turned back to Mr. Bender angrily. "Get your class under control!" he barked.

"Consider that done," Mr. Bender answered, breathing a sigh of relief. He was not thrilled about facing a bunch of near-rioting teenagers. But he would choose them over Dean Rivers any day.

"Your little Webcast has disrupted the entire campus of Pacific Coast Academy." Dean Rivers stood in his office, dressed in a dark suit and red tie. Behind him, floor-to-ceiling windows showed off the jewel that was "his" school: a gorgeous campus with its amazing staff and its usually well-mannered student body.

Chase and Michael looked at the dean sheepishly. But Chase could not keep quiet. How could their tiny Webcast have disrupted the *entire* school? It was preposterous. "Sir . . ."

"Be quiet!" the dean barked.

Michael leaned closer to Chase. "You should be quiet," he said under his breath.

"I'll be quiet," Chase agreed in a low tone. The dean did not appear to be in a discussing sort of mood.

"We don't need this kind of trouble here at PCA. So I'm putting a stop to it," the dean announced.

Chase was not entirely clear. "And by 'a stop' you mean . . ."

"Your Webcast is canceled," the dean said slowly.

"What?" Chase was outraged.

"That's censorship!" Michael protested.

"Yeah, we have a right to free speech!" Chase was yelling now, but the dean did not appear to notice. He was picking up the phone on his desk and dialing.

"You can't just cancel our Webcast!" Michael argued.

A moment later both boys were being escorted out of the office door by the dean's assistant.

Chase was stunned.

Michael shook his head in disbelief. "He just canceled our Webcast!"

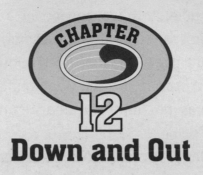

Down and Out

Zoey strolled across campus on her way to her dorm, thinking about what a jerk Logan was. How could he possibly think that girls were too emotional to have powerful jobs? Ugh! She was getting mad all over again just thinking about it when she spotted Chase lying on a hammock in the shade. And the weird thing was, he was lying facedown. Zoey walked up to the hammock, stopping right next to it. "Chase?" she said.

"Hey," Chase replied in a monotone.

"What are you doing?" Zoey asked.

"Lying here, on a hammock," Chase said. Wasn't it obvious?

"Are you gonna turn over and talk to me?" Zoey asked. This looked bad. She had never seen Chase looking so, um, down before.

Chase didn't move. "No."

"Why not?"

"I'm depressed," Chase said, still not moving.

"Okay," Zoey said, thinking. She had to help her friend. She took off her khaki-colored backpack. The charms she'd used to decorate it chimed as she dropped it, then lay down on the ground underneath the hammock, looking up. Now, at least, she could see her friend's face.

"Boo!" she said, trying to cheer him up.

"Hello," Chase said woodenly, though he had to admit it was great to see Zoey's face.

"Want a grape?" Zoey offered her favorite food with a smile.

A grape sounded good, but Chase didn't have the energy to get up. "Feed me?" he asked.

Zoey reached up and popped a grape through the hammock webbing into Chase's mouth. "I'm sorry Dean Rivers canceled your show," she said. She knew it was what was getting Chase down.

"Yeah, me too," Chase agreed.

Zoey took a breath. "I feel like it's all my fault," she added.

"Come on," Chase said. "Before you and Logan came on our Webcast only, like, nine people watched it. And we had almost hit three hundred last night because of you guys." He paused. Three hundred! But then... "I can't believe Dean Rivers just canceled us."

"I know!" Zoey agreed. "It's censorship!" Whenever she thought about it, she got mad. It was totally unfair and wrong!

"That's what we told him," Chase said. "Grape," he added. Zoey popped another grape into Chase's mouth. He wasn't sure if it was Zoey or the grapes, but he was starting to feel a little bit better. "Oh, hey," he said, reaching into his back pocket. He pulled out a DVD and handed it to Zoey.

"A DVD?" Zoey asked curiously.

Chase nodded. "Yeah, I burned our last two shows on there for you. It's good stuff ... especially you and Logan. You should watch it."

Zoey sighed as she stared at the DVD. It was such a bummer that the show was canceled! And no matter what Chase said, she still felt responsible.

Chase looked down at Zoey. He could tell that she felt pretty bad. .... She was just staring at the disk he'd handed her. "To watch it, you know, you have to put it in a machine hooked up to a TV set," he joked.

Zoey smirked. "Thank you, Chase," she said slyly.

She popped a final grape into her friend's mouth and got to her feet.

Chase stared down at the grass where Zoey's head used to be. He was still totally bummed about his show. But talking to Zoey had helped — a lot.

Across campus in Quinn's room, the giant television screen displayed a dizzying array of psychedelic colors and patterns. Pink, purple, and blue dots swirled on the walls, the furniture — even on the three girls in the room!

Nicole sat on the bed, staring intently at the television screen, her expression blank.

Quinn put a knee on the bed and leaned in close to Nicole's ear. "Nicole," she said, chantlike. "Do you hear me? If you hear me, respond."

Nicole's eyes never left the swirling screen. "I hear you," she said distantly.

Quinn smiled. So far, it was working! She looked over at Lola standing on the other side of the bed. "Okay, she's ready," she whispered. "Go for it."

Lola stepped close to Nicole's other side, leaning on the bed. "Right," she said softly. The bright circles moved across her black T-shirt and chunky orange-and-green beaded necklace. "Nicole, listen to me carefully," Lola said slowly.

"Listen to her carefully," Quinn repeated with a small nod.

Lola leaned around Nicole and shot Quinn a look. What was she, a parrot? Clearing her throat lightly, she got back to the task at hand: hypnotizing Nicole. She leaned in close to Nicole's ear while the whirling dots moved across the dazed girl's pale green top.

"In your algebra class, there are many cute guys," Lola intoned.

"*Soooo* cute," Nicole said longingly.

"But now, when you look at them, you won't see them for who they are," Lola instructed. "You will see them as . . ." She paused, not sure who Nicole should see them as. She leaned around Nicole, silently asking Quinn for some advice. Quinn shook her head, making her long hair fall over her shoulders. She had no idea, either. Lola thought fast. She had to come up with something so she could finish her instructions. ". . . your grandfather."

Quinn raised an eyebrow. That seemed like a weird choice. "Her grandfather?" she whispered.

Lola shrugged. She didn't hear Quinn offering up any better ideas!

"My grandfather," Nicole said with a distant smile. "Paw Paw."

Lola made a face. "Paw Paw," she said, surprised.

Quinn's nose wrinkled up as if she was examining an experiment gone horribly wrong. "Eew," she said as the screen in front of them continued to swirl.

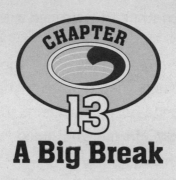

CHAPTER 13

A Big Break

Zoey, Chase, Logan, and Michael were having lunch at their regular outdoor table. The mood was still glum, but Zoey was determined to do what she could to make things better — for all of them. She was about to take a bite of salad when a cool-looking guy in a blazer approached their table.

"Excuse me, Zoey Brooks?" he asked.

"Yeah," Zoey replied with a nod.

"Hi, I'm Jesse Freeman, producer over at K Coast channel seven," he said with a smile.

"No way," Zoey said, excited. What was he doing on the PCA campus?

"Wait, K Coast the TV station?" Logan asked.

"Yeah." Jesse said. "You watch some of our shows?"

"No," Logan replied. "They're lame."

"Dude," Michael said, whacking him on the shoulder. Logan had to be the rudest kid on the planet.

"Yeah, dude,". Zoey agreed. *Hello!* This guy was from the local TV station, and he wanted to talk to them!

"That's okay, I'm not offended," Jesse said, sitting down. "That much."

"So, you got the DVD?" Zoey asked with a smile.

"I did." Jesse nodded.

"What DVD?" Chase asked. As usual, he had no idea what was going on. "You sent him the DVD?"

"Yes, we already covered that," Zoey said to Chase, feeling a little exasperated. A television producer was sitting at their table! Could the guys just let her talk to him for a second — or did they have to keep interrupting to embarrass themselves? "So, what did you think?" Zoey asked with a grin.

"I thought the show was really terrific," Jesse said. "And it might be a good way for K Coast to build up our teen audience."

Zoey gasped. "On TV?"

"Yes. You'd be seen by an audience of over *fifty thousand people.*" He stated the number slowly for emphasis.

"Deal!" Zoey said.

"Deal?" Logan repeated questioningly. They hadn't even discussed the terms yet! And Logan was not about to work for free. . . .

"Yeah," Michael said. "Simple word, four letters."

"Yeah, now be quiet," Chase instructed. This was looking good and Logan had better not mess it up!

"Just have a teacher bring you down to the studio at four-thirty on Monday, and I'll take care of the rest," Jesse said. "Sound good?"

"Sounds awesome!" Zoey said excitedly.

Jesse got to his feet and held out his hand. "Well then, see you Monday."

Zoey grinned and shook his hand. "Yeah, you will," she promised.

Everyone else got to their feet as Jesse walked away. As soon as he was across the lawn, Chase turned to Zoey. "You are amazing!" he said gratefully.

"Yes, I could kiss you!" Michael cheered, putting his hands on Zoey's shoulders.

"Yeah, me too," Logan said, inching his way closer.

Chase put up a protective arm, forcing Logan back. "Okay, you know what?" he asked. "I'm sure we

94

would all like to kiss Zoey, but we have a TV show to plan!" He pumped his fists in the air.

"Yeah!"

"Yes!"

"Woo-hoo!"

The three cheered and took off toward the guys' dorm to get to work. But three seconds later they were back at their table snatching up their drinks. Creativity was thirsty work!

In algebra class, Nicole listened carefully to her teacher and made notes in her notebook.

"So to solve the problem, you need to multiply both sides by the square root of the original figure." Her teacher gestured to the equations on the board with his pointer.

Ahead of her in the next row, Lance McAllister turned around and flashed her an adorable smile.

Nicole tilted her head to the side and smiled back. But then Lance's totally cute face morphed into a bald, wrinkly mess. Her grandfather!

"Nicole, come give Grandpa a big old hug!" he said.

Nicole stared in horror at the image of her grandfather, then shivered. Ugh!

"And then you take the Y coordinate . . ." Nicole got back to her note taking. She was concentrating just fine.

Until Daniel James turned and gave her a flirty nod. Nicole twirled her hair through her fingers and beamed. But then Daniel's face disappeared, replaced by an old man's with a beaky nose.

"Nicole," her imaginary grandfather called. "Come help Grandpa do his laundry."

Nicole stared at the horrible vision in front of her and shuddered. What was happening?

Finally the cutest boy in the class, Harry Matthau, turned around and smiled right at her. Nicole sat back and gave him her cutest look. But before she saw his reaction, Harry was gone, and in his spot was her aging grandfather!

"Nicole," he called in singsong. "Go get Grandpa his special ointment."

Eeewwww! Nicole screwed her face up and leaned forward to get a better look. This was waaay too freaky — and gross!

"Nicole!" a voice boomed out from the front of the room.

Nicole shook off the horrible visions, sat up

straight, and looked up at her teacher. "Um, yes?" she asked in a small voice.

"Are you distracted?" he asked point blank.

"Um, no, not anymore," she said firmly. "Let's just focus on algebra." Anything to keep her grandfather out of her classroom!

CHAPTER 14

Speaking Out

Downtown, Zoey, Chase, Logan, and Michael were heading into K Coast. Zoey was so excited, she couldn't keep the giant smile off her face — and didn't try very hard. This was extremely cool!

Behind her, Chase checked everything out. This was a totally new experience for him. "A real TV studio!" he said, practically jumping up and down. "Can you believe it?" Michael nodded and slipped his co-creator a low five.

"Hey, guys," Jesse called out to them as he crossed the studio. He held his arms out in a friendly greeting. "Welcome to K Coast." He shook hands with Chase and Michael.

"Listen," Logan said, interrupting the cozy meeting. They had to get a few things straight. "I'm gonna need my hair and makeup done," he stated.

Zoey rolled her eyes. Logan was lucky Chase and Michael were in between them, or she'd clock him. What did he think he was doing, making demands like that?

But Jesse took it in stride. "We have people for that," he said casually.

Logan nodded. "Good." His dad was in the biz, and he didn't want anyone at K Coast to think he was small-time.

"So, uh, where should we set up our stuff?" Chase asked.

Jesse looked a bit baffled. "What stuff?" he asked.

"We brought some props for the comedy bits we do," Michael said, gesturing to Chase's backpack excitedly. They were about to do those bits on TV! He'd gotten his "professional" nose trimmer "professionally" sharpened for the occasion.

"Um, okay," Jesse said hesitantly. "I guess I wasn't clear when we talked back at PCA," he admitted.

"Not clear about what?" Zoey asked. She was getting an uneasy feeling.

"Well, uh, we're only interested in putting Zoey and Logan on K Coast," he said, looking a little sheepish.

"But it's *The Chase and Michael Show*," Zoey pointed out.

"And we're kinda Chase and Michael," Chase added, gesturing to himself and his roommate.

Michael raised his hand awkwardly. "Michael."

"Chase."

"Hello."

"Hello." Chase tried to smile, but he suddenly had a lump in his stomach.

"Listen, I'm really sorry," Jesse said. He sounded sorry enough. But Zoey wasn't sure that was good enough.

She looked around the studio, unsure what to do next. She spotted a big ZOEY AND LOGAN banner on the wall and her stomach flipped. Now she knew what to do. She turned to Jesse. "Okay, you know what? We're not interested," she said flatly.

"Um, yes, we are," Logan objected.

"Not without Chase and Michael," Zoey insisted. The whole thing was their idea!

Logan could not let it go so easily. "This face belongs on television," he said, pointing to his flawless visage. Um, hello!

"Look, there's no way —" Zoey began.

"Whoa," Chase said, taking Zoey by the arm. He gently pushed her backward so they could talk alone

100

for a minute. Sure, Chase was bummed. But there was no need for Zoey to throw everything away because of him and Michael.

Zoey stood her ground. "We're not doing this without you and Michael," she insisted.

"Look, that's really sweet and all," Chase admitted. He was sincerely touched. "But they don't *want* us."

"But it's *your* show."

Chase shook his curly dark head. "No. Dean Rivers canceled our show. But you guys have a really cool shot here. And . . . I want you to take it."

Zoey stared at Chase, her best guy friend in the world. He was speaking the truth. And if he wanted her to do it . . .

Half an hour later Zoey and Logan were sitting in the chairs on the set of the Zoey and Logan show.

"First positions," a crew member called.

"Roll camera," said someone else.

"Rolling," came the reply.

And the countdown began.

In the girls' lounge, several PCA students were waiting for the show to come on. Nicole dashed in at the last second — she'd just finished her algebra homework.

"Has it started yet?" she asked.

"It's about to," Lola replied, adjusting her beret and leaning forward.

On the screen in the front of the room, the girls could see Zoey and Logan sitting in two orange butterfly chairs. "And now, live in the afternoon, 'He Says, She Says,' with your hosts Zoey Brooks and Logan Reese!"

The girls gave a little cheer.

"Oh, there they are!" Quinn squealed.

Lola clapped her hands together. She was so excited, she was barely even jealous that Zoey was on the small screen without her! She hoped the girl had acting chops.

"Where are Chase and Michael?" Nicole asked, wrinkling her nose in confusion. Wasn't it supposed to be *The Chase and Michael Show*?

Lola and Quinn shrugged. They had no idea.

Logan smiled cheesily at the camera. "Hello, my name is Logan Reese," he said smoothly.

"And I'm Zoey Brooks," Zoey added, looking kind of . . . annoyed.

"And today, we're going to talk about some interesting topics," Logan said enthusiastically, glancing down at the notebook in his hands. "First . . . girls and sports." He paused to smile for the camera, hoping it was getting his good side. Then he smiled even bigger. Of course it was! All of his sides were good. . . .

"Now, I think it's fine if girls want to have their own little sports teams." He waggled his fingers to show how trivial girls' sports were. "But they should not be able to play on the guys' teams!"

The students in the PCA girls' lounge groaned. Typical Logan. He never learned, and he could be such a jerk!

"Zoey?" Logan asked with a cocky smile, waiting for her to take the bait.

Zoey stared at the camera, feeling annoyed. "Yeah, I think you're right," she said, even though she didn't agree at all. She was still so frustrated that Chase and Michael's show was canceled and K Coast didn't want them, she had no fight left in her for Logan and his big head.

"Huh?" Logan said, dumbfounded. Why wasn't she arguing with him? She was Zoey Brooks, right?

"I said, you're right," Zoey repeated. Was he hard of hearing?

"Uh, okay . . . Let's move on to our next topic, then," Logan said, scanning his list for another subject to discuss. "Oh, yeah. Ordering at restaurants. I say girls take way too long to order food. 'Ooooh, I'm a girl. I'll have the chopped salad, but I want the lettuce on the side. Nah, nah, nah, nah, nah,'" he said in an irritating nasal voice. "Guys, it's just, like, 'Give me a cheeseburger,' end of story. Zoey?"

Zoey shrugged. Did anybody really care about how people ordered food in restaurants? Couldn't they talk about something that actually mattered? "I agree," she said, just to close the subject.

"What is she doing?" Michael whispered to Chase from off camera. She was throwing the show!

Chase shrugged. He didn't know why Zoey was not being her regular self. Normally she didn't let Logan get away with any of his insulting behavior.

Nobody in the girls' lounge at PCA knew what to think, either.

"Why isn't Zoey fighting back?" Quinn asked, tossing her head in frustration. Next to her, Lola shook her head. This was weird.

Logan glared at Zoey. She was ruining his chance to be on TV again! "Okay, for our next topic, let's talk about . . . eating kittens!" he said through clenched teeth. "I feel that people should eat more kittens! Little itty-bitty-bitty kittens for breakfast. You agree with that, Zoey?" he challenged hotly, waving his hands in the air before sitting back to hear her response.

"You want to know what I'd like to talk about?" Zoey asked.

"Yes!" Logan replied. Anything, as long as she spoke more than three words!

"Censorship."

"Good!" Logan agreed. Now they were getting somewhere. But . . . he leaned in close to Zoey. "What's censorship?" he whispered.

"Censorship is when somebody stops you from saying what you want to say," she told Logan. Then she turned to the camera. "And that's what happened to my friends Chase and Michael," she told the viewers.

"Uh, Zoey . . ." This was not any better. Logan tried to steer her back on track.

Zoey ignored him. "Camera lady, show Chase and Michael," she prodded the camerawoman.

The camerawoman turned the camera so that the audience could see the two guys sitting backstage.

"Hello." Chase waved awkwardly.

Michael did a round wave, like a mime. "How do," he greeted.

"Chase and Michael go to Pacific Coast Academy with me," Zoey explained when the camera was back on her. "And they had this really cool Webcast."

"Zoey!" Logan interrupted.

"Shhhh!" Zoey shushed him. "And the dean banned it. And I say that's censorship, which is wrong." She got to her feet. "And if you agree, go to PCA and tell Dean Rivers how you feel about censorship."

The girls' lounge erupted into cheers. "Go, Zoey!" Nicole shouted as Lola and Quinn slapped each other a mid-five.

Things were not so cheerful at K Coast.

"And . . . that's a commercial," the camera-woman said.

Jesse looked hard at Zoey. "What was that?" he asked.

"Yeah," Logan agreed, throwing down his note-book in frustration. "Are you insane?" he asked her.

Zoey was about to answer when Chase and Michael rushed up to her. "Zoey, that was great!" Chase said triumphantly. "You just told, like, fifty thousand people what Dean Rivers did."

"I know!" Zoey said with a huge grin. She hadn't planned it, but talking about censorship just seemed like the right thing to do. And it felt great!

"Do you know what's gonna happen?" Michael asked excitedly. He wasn't exactly sure, but he had a pretty good idea. . . .

*   *   *

Within an hour, a mob of angry kids was gathered outside Dean Rivers's office. They shouted and waved signs that read things like DOWN WITH RIVERS and END CENSORSHIP NOW.

Dean Rivers scowled at the mob and stepped outside to shoo them away. "Will you kids get out of here?" he shouted. Someone threw a rotten tomato and it sailed past him, hitting the large glass window. Dean Rivers ducked back inside the door, then emerged again. "Who let you onto this campus?" he demanded as another overripe tomato slammed into the door he was half hiding behind. "Am I going to have to call the police?" *Thud.* The tomatoes were getting close. Too close.

Dean Rivers ducked back into his office and closed the door just as his assistant came into the room. "Dean Rivers, I have Zoey and Logan here," she said.

Dean Rivers pushed off the door frame and adjusted his suit jacket. "Send them in," he said.

Zoey walked nervously into the dean's office with Logan right behind her.

"Zoey and Logan." Dean Rivers spoke their names as if they described something completely disgusting.

"Hi, Dean Rivers," Zoey said sheepishly.

"How ya doin'?" Logan added.

"How am I doing?" Dean Rivers repeated. He turned and gestured to the angry mob on the other side of the glass. "Those are tomatoes!" he bellowed, waving a finger at the red smears on the window and door. "That is a waste of lycopene!"

Zoey was tempted to run, but she had to speak her mind. "Well, people get really upset about censorship," she pointed out quietly.

"Just make them go away!" he ordered.

"I'm sure they'll leave if you let Chase and Michael have their show back," she suggested with a tiny shrug.

"No," Dean Rivers said flatly, raising his chin. "I will not be pushed around."

Logan shrugged. "You'd better tell them," he suggested.

"Oh, I'll tell them," Dean Rivers vowed. He turned and shoved the door open.

"All right, you people," he said. "I am in charge of this school! And Chase and Michael cannot have their show back!" *Splat!* A giant tomato slammed into Dean Rivers's jacket lapel and dripped down his suit. *Wham!* A second one hit him in the face.

Dean Rivers slowly stepped back into his office and closed the door. And then, even more slowly, he turned to face Zoey and Logan. Tomato juice and seeds covered his shirt, jacket, and half his face. It dripped onto his shoes.

"Tell Chase and Michael they can have their show back," he said quietly.

Zoey grinned. She was sorry that Dean Rivers had to get tomatoes thrown at him, but if that was what it took . . .

As soon as Zoey left the dean's office, she went to find Chase and Michael. It didn't take long. Chase was waiting in one of the quads. Zoey rushed up to him and told him the news.

"Seriously?" Chase asked, totally psyched.

"Seriously," Zoey confirmed with a grin.

"We got our show back!" Michael cried, rushing up to them. He was slapping hands with Chase as Logan and the girls rushed up. There were more cheers and hugs all around.

"Zoey, you were so awesome on the show today," Nicole congratulated her.

Zoey smiled. She wasn't trying to be awesome — she was just trying to do the right thing. "Thanks," she replied.

Lola gave Nicole a nudge. "Harry Matthau walking

this way," she said under her breath. And he was making a beeline right for Nicole.

Nicole smoothed her skirt and her hair and tried to look as cute as possible.

"Hey, Nicole," Harry said. "Me and some guys are going to catch a movie on campus later. Wanna come?"

Nicole beamed at the invitation. Did she ever! "Yeah, I'd . . ." She started to accept, but suddenly Harry was gone, and her grandpa was standing in front of her instead, stooped, bald, and old. "Nicole," he called in his scratchy voice. "Help me take out my teeth."

Nicole's perky smiling expression curdled into a look of disgust. "Eewww!" she shrieked, waving her arms in a panic. Paw Paw was everywhere! She ducked behind her friends and rushed down the path.

Lola and Quinn chuckled and Michael gave Harry a sympathetic pat on the shoulder.

"Later," Logan called casually as Chase gave Harry a "maybe next time" look.

But Harry didn't notice. He was too busy wondering what had just happened. "What'd I say?" he asked himself as he stumbled away.